What Mommy Really Means

Written by Beth Thurman
Illustrated by Valerie Bouthyette

To order additional copies of this book, contact:
Xlibris Corporation
1-888-795-4274
www.Xlibris.com
Orders@Xlibris.com

What Mommy **Really** Means

Written by
Beth Thurman

Illustrated by Valerie Bouthyette

To Gray and Porter:

Mommy wishes she could communicate this well.
I love you, now go to sleep.

Mommy says, "It's time to get up."

Mommy means, "It's a brand new day
and you are going to have great adventures."

Mommy says, "Finish your oatmeal."

Mommy means, "Just like race cars need fuel,
you need energy for the day."

Mommy says, "Brush your teeth."

Mommy means, "You don't want them to turn brown and fall out, like the *crocodile in the zoo*."

Mommy says, "Time for school."

Mommy means, "You are very smart
and someday you will *do great things.*"

Mommy says, "Hold my hand."

Mommy means, "The world is a
fascinating place, let me guide you."

Mommy says, "Share your things."

Mommy means, "It is more fun to play with friends, than to play all by yourself."

Mommy says, "Eat your veggies."

Mommy means, "They will give you superpowers to soar to new heights."

Mommy says, "Take a bath."

Mommy means, "Bubbles wash the dirt
and day's disappointments away."

Mommy says, "Time for bed."

Mommy means, "Sleep brings
dreams of faraway and fantastic places."

Mommy says, "I love you."

Mommy means, "You are my whole world and no matter how big you grow, I will always be your mommy."

There is a universal set of functional things that mothers say to their children. We all wish we could convey the full meaning in our words. Here's hoping this helps your kids figure you out!

CPSIA information can be obtained
at www.ICGtesting.com
Printed in the USA
264301LV00006B